MOONBEAM
AND THE
CAPTAIN

SELMA AND JACK
WASSERMANN

ILLUSTRATIONS
GEORGE ROHRER

BENEFIC PRESS
WESTCHESTER, ILLINOIS

The Moonbeam Books

Copyright 1968 by Benefic Press
All Rights Reserved
Printed in the United States of America

Library of Congress
Number 68-18211

CONTENTS

Moonbeam and the Captain

This is Moonbeam.

Moonbeam is a chimp.

Mr. Green is with her.

"Come on, Moonbeam,"
said Mr. Green.

"This is the ship."

"Heen, hon, hon, hoon,"
said Moonbeam.

"Up you go!" said Mr. Green.

Moonbeam was soon on the ship
with Mr. Green.

Moonbeam and Mr. Green went
to see the Captain.

The Captain looked at Moonbeam.

"A chimp?" he said.

"A chimp on this ship?
That can be trouble!"

Moonbeam did not like that.

"Heen! Heeeeen!" she said.

7

"Moonbeam is not like other chimps," said Mr. Green.

"She is a moon chimp.

One day she will go to the moon!"

"Chimps like to play," said the Captain.

"I can not have a chimp playing on this ship!"

"Moonbeam will be
good," said Mr. Green.

"You will have
to see to that,"
the Captain said.

"I will,"
said Mr. Green.

Moonbeam looked at
the Captain.

"Heeeen!" she said.

Moonbeam went out with Mr. Green.

Down in the ship they went.

"You will have to be good, Moonbeam," said Mr. Green.

"Heen!" said Moonbeam.

"Heen! Heen!"

Soon Mr. Green said,

"Here we are!"

He went in with Moonbeam.

"We will like it

in here," he said.

Bobo

Moonbeam looked out
of the ship.

She saw a mother and
a father.

She saw a boy.

And she saw a chimp!

"Come on, John," said the
mother to the boy.

"The ship will go soon."

"And Bobo?" said the boy.

"Bobo can not come,"
said the father.

"This ship is not for chimps,
John."

John did not like that.

John looked at Bobo.

He said something to the chimp.

The boy's mother and father
did not see what he did.

"We will have to go, John,"
they said.

Soon they went up
on the ship.

Moonbeam looked
at the other chimp.

She saw Bobo come to the ship
and jump up on it!

No one saw Bobo.

"Hon? Hon, hon, hon?"
said Moonbeam.

"What is it, Moonbeam?"
said Mr. Green.

Up went Bobo.

"Heen, hon, hon!" said Moonbeam.

Mr. Green went to have a look.

Bobo was in the ship.

Mr. Green did not see Bobo.

Mr. Green did see something.

It was the ship.

"Look, Moonbeam!" he said.

"You can see the ship go!"

Moonbeam looked out.

She saw the ship come away.

"Hoon, hon, hon, heen!"

she said.

Up and Down

"Come, Moonbeam," said Mr. Green.

"We will have a look
at this ship."

Moonbeam went with Mr. Green.

Soon they saw John.

John looked at Moonbeam
and Mr. Green.

John did not stop.

This is where
John went.
"No one
can see what
I have here,"
he said.
What was John
up to?

It was Bobo!

"Look!" said John.

"I have something for you to eat."

Bobo liked it.

"Ung-ung!" he said.

"I will have to go," said John.

"Be good!"

The ship went on and on.

Moonbeam looked up.

What was this?

She looked out.

She did not like what she saw.

Up went the ship!

Up went Moonbeam!

Down went the ship!

Down went Moonbeam!

She did not like it.

"Heeeeeeeeen!" she said.

Up and down went the ship.

Out came Bobo.

And away he went.

Trouble for Moonbeam

Day came.

Moonbeam went up

with Mr. Green.

She did not look good.

"Heeeeeeeeen!" she said.

Mr. Green looked at Moonbeam.

Moonbeam looked down at the ship.

"Heen! Heen!" she said.

They did not see the other chimp!

Moonbeam and Mr. Green went on.
Soon the Captain came.
"Come," he said to Mr. Green.
"I have something for you to see."

Moonbeam and Mr. Green went
with the Captain.

"Look, Mr. Green,"
said the Captain.

"Look at what this chimp did."

"Heen!" said Moonbeam.

"Heen! Heen!"

Mr. Green looked at Moonbeam.

"Was it you?" he said.

"Heeeeeeeen!" said Moonbeam.

"Chimps eat this,"
said the Captain.
"Chimps are not
good to have
on a ship."
Mr. Green did
not like this.
"Come on,
Moonbeam," he said.
"We are in trouble
with the Captain."
They went out.

"You will have to be in here,
Moonbeam," said Mr. Green.

"You can not go out."

"Heen!" said Moonbeam.

"You will have no trouble
with the Captain in here,"
said Mr. Green.

"Something Is on this Ship"

A day came and went.

The ship went on and on.

Mr. Green saw the Captain.

"What is it, Captain?"

he said.

"Look at this!"
said the Captain.

"You see?" said Mr. Green.

"It was not Moonbeam!"

"Something is on this ship,"
said the Captain.

"Something that eats!"

"What can it be?"
said Mr. Green.

"We will have to look for it,"
said the Captain.

The Captain looked.

Mr. Green looked.

Others looked.

They looked
and looked.

"Look!" said Mr. Green.

"It was here!"

The others ran to see.

"Where?" said the Captain.

"It was here," said Mr. Green,

"and it went away."

The Captain looked at Mr. Green.

"You and the others go on,"
he said.

"Go on looking.

I will be with you soon."

Chimp on the Run

The Captain went in here.

"Ung, ung, ung, ung,"
said something.

"What is this?"
said the Captain.

"Ung, ung! Ung, ung!"
it said.

Up jumped the Captain!

Out jumped Bobo!

And away he ran!

The Captain ran out.

"Stop that chimp!" he said.

"Stop it!"

Mr. Green and the others soon came.

"Look at Moonbeam go!" they said.

"That chimp is not Moonbeam."
said Mr. Green.

Bobo ran.

The Captain ran.

Mr. Green ran.

The others ran.

John saw Bobo and the others.

He did not like what he saw.

Bobo saw the
Captain come.

The Captain ran
to Bobo.

"Stop, you chimp!"
he said.

Bobo did not
like it.

And up he jumped.

Up and up went Bobo.

The Captain and the others

came to a stop.

They looked up at the chimp.

"We can not go up

where that chimp is," they said.

"Good Work, Moonbeam!"

"Come down here!"
said the Captain.

Bobo did not come down.

"Come on down," said Mr. Green.

Bobo looked at the Captain.

He did not come down.

Mr. Green looked
at the Captain.
"I have it!"
he said.
"We will soon
have that chimp
down here!"

Mr. Green ran.
Down in the ship
he went.

"Come on Moonbeam,"
said Mr. Green.

"You will see something
that you will like!"

Moonbeam came
with Mr. Green.

Up in the ship
they went.

"Look up, Moonbeam!"
said Mr. Green.

Moonbeam looked up.

It was the other chimp!

"Hoon! Hoon!" said Moonbeam.

"Come on down, chimp!"
said Mr. Green.

"Here is Moonbeam
to play with you!"

Bobo looked at Moonbeam.

It was good to have a chimp
to play with.

Down he came!

The Captain looked
at Moonbeam and Bobo.

"Chimps! Chimps! Chimps!"
he said.

"You will see," said Mr. Green.

"Moonbeam and Bobo will play.

And John can be with the chimps.

That will stop the chimp trouble

on this ship."

"Good! Good!" said John.

"Hoon! Hoon!" said Moonbeam.

"Ung! Ung!" said Bobo.

"Bah!" said the Captain.

And away he went.

VOCABULARY

The total vocabulary of this book is 64 words, excluding proper names and sound words. The 44 words in roman type should be familiar to children reading on a pre-primer level. The 20 words above pre-primer level are shown in italic type. The numbers indicate the pages on which the words first appear.

a 5
and 5
are 11
at 7
away 23

be 9
boy 23

came 23
can 29
captain 7
chimp 5
come 6

day 24
did 7
down 10

eat 20

father 12
for 13

go 6
good 10

have 16
he 11

her 5
here 11

I 8
in 10
is 5
it 11

jumped 37

like 7
look 16

moon 8
mother 12

no 15
not 7

on 6
one 8
out 10
other 45

play 8

ran 34

said 6
saw 12
see 7
she 8
ship 6
something 17
soon 11
stop 38

that 7
the 6
they 10
this 5
to 7
trouble 29

up 6

was 6
we 14
went 7
what 14
where 19
will 8
with 5

you 6